Family Storybook Library

# Your Place in
# the Circle of Life

Stories About Courage and Responsibility

BOOK SEVEN

# Your Place in the Circle of Life

Stories About Courage and Responsibility

# Introduction

Children often daydream about being rulers,
but few stop to think about the courage and sense
of responsibility required to be a just and fair leader.
Yes, being in charge has perks, but it also comes with
a heavy price. Leading effectively means putting others'
needs before your own; it means considering the
well-being of many before making decisions; it means
keeping your judgment clear and free from prejudice.

Although he struggles against his preordained path,
Simba eventually acknowledges his sense of duty and
accepts his responsibilities as the Lion King. Cinderella,
despite her delayed royal fate, remains kind, courteous,
and friendly to those around her. Both display the
qualities integral to their true calling.

# Born to Be King

from *The Lion King*

⬤⬤⬤

*You can't change the past, but you can improve the future.*

ne day, Nala, an old friend of Simba, appeared in the jungle and begged Simba to return to Pride Rock, where Scar, Simba's wicked uncle, had assumed the place of king.

"I can't go back," Simba insisted. "Look, sometimes bad things happen, and there's nothing you can do about it. So why worry?"

Simba told Nala he couldn't help her and walked away.

That night, Simba wandered across a high grassy plain. *What would it prove if I went back*

to *Pride Rock?* he thought. *It won't change anything. You can't change the past.*

As Simba roamed, a baboon jumped out of a tree and followed him. "Will you stop following me?" Simba growled. "Who are you?"

Rafiki said, "The question is: Who are you?"

"I thought I knew." Simba sighed. "But now I'm not so sure."

Rafiki chuckled. "I know who you are. You're Mufasa's boy."

"You knew my father?" Simba asked, amazed.

"Correction!" Rafiki replied. "I *know* your father."

Simba shook his head sadly. "I hate to tell you this, but he died a long time ago."

"Nope!" the baboon chortled. "Wrong again! He's alive. I'll show him to you. You follow old Rafiki. He knows the way!"

Simba followed Rafiki to a pool. Rafiki parted the reeds and said, "Shh. Look down there."

Simba peered into the water, hoping to see a miracle. "That's not my father," he said quietly. "That's just my reflection."

"No," Rafiki insisted. "Look *harder*."

Simba tried. It was true that he looked like Mufasa, but . . .

"See?" said Rafiki. "Your father lives in you."

Then Simba heard Mufasa's regal voice booming from the heavens. He looked up at the stars.

"Simba," commanded Mufasa, "you must take your place in the circle of life. Remember who you are. You are my son, and the one true king. Remember . . . remember . . ."

As the voice faded, Rafiki winked and

said, "What was that? The weather . . . very peculiar!"

"Looks like the winds are changing," said Simba.

"Change is good!" replied Rafiki.

"Yeah," said Simba, "but it's not easy. I know what I have to do, but going back means that I'll have to face my past. I've been running from it for so long."

Rafiki lifted his cane and hit Simba on the head.

"Ow!" cried Simba. "What was that for?"

Rafiki laughed. "It doesn't matter. It's in the past!"

"Yeah," said Simba, rubbing his head, "but it still hurts."

"Oh, yes, the past can hurt, but the way I see it, you either run from it . . . or learn from it."

Simba was convinced. He ran through the tall grass, heading for Pride Rock. He *would* challenge Scar. It was time.

# Fit for a Princess

from *Cinderella*

*Don't be afraid to make yourself heard.*

**T**he morning after the ball, Cinderella gazed longingly at the glass slipper, her only reminder of the wonderful time she had spent at the ball. Thanks to her fairy godmother, Cinderella had left her household chores behind and spent one

perfect, magical night dancing with a handsome stranger.

When Cinderella heard her stepmother calling, she put the slipper away and hurried downstairs.

As Cinderella stood at the door, she heard her stepmother say to her stepsisters, "The Grand Duke has been hunting all night for the girl who lost her slipper at the ball. The Duke has been ordered to try the glass slipper on every girl in the kingdom, and if the one can be found whose foot fits the slipper, then that girl shall be the Prince's bride!"

Cinderella forgot all about her chores. Last night she had been dancing with the Prince! "I must get dressed," she murmured. "It would never do for the Duke to see me like this. . . ."

Having overheard her, the stepmother

knew then that Cinderella had been the girl
at the ball. She followed Cinderella upstairs
and locked her in her room.

The Grand Duke soon arrived. Anastasia was the first to try on the slipper. "I knew it was my slipper!" she said to the footman. "It's exactly my size." The slipper barely fit over Anastasia's toes. "Oh, well," sputtered Anastasia, "it may be a trifle snug today. You know how it is, dancing all night . . . it's always fit before!"

The Grand Duke sniffed, not believing a word, and asked Drizella to try on the slipper. "Get away from me," she snapped at the footman. "I'll make it fit!"

But nothing Drizella did could make the slipper fit.

As the Grank Duke prepared to leave, Cinderella flew down the stairs. Her friends, the mice, had stolen the key to her room from the stepmother's pocket and freed her.

"May I try on the slipper?" Cinderella
cried out. As the footman approached, the
stepmother stuck out her cane and tripped

him. The glass slipper crashed to the floor and shattered.

The Grand Duke exclaimed, "This is terrible! What will the King say? What will he do?"

Cinderella said, "But perhaps, I can help . . ."

"Nothing can help now," moaned the Grand Duke, his head in his hands.

"But you see," said Cinderella, reaching into her pocket, "I have the other slipper."

The Grand Duke placed the glass slipper on Cinderella's foot. To his delight, it fit perfectly!

And so Cinderella was taken to the palace, where she and the Prince lived happily ever after.